There, There

written by
Tim Beiser

illustrated by
Bill Slavin

TUNDRA BOOKS

Tundra Books, a division of Random House of Canada Limited, a Penguin Random House Company

LIBRARY AND ARCHIVES CANADA CATALOGUING IN PUBLICATION

Beiser, Tim, 1959–, author
      There, there / Tim Beiser ; illustrated by Bill Slavin.

Issued in print and electronic formats.
ISBN 978-1-77049-752-8 (hardback).—978-1-77049-754-2 (epub)

      I. Slavin, Bill, illustrator II. Title.

PS8603.E42846T44 2017   jC813'.6   C2016-902546-2
                                                 C2016-902547-0

Published simultaneously in the United States of America by Tundra Books of Northern New York,
a division of Random House of Canada Limited, a Penguin Random House Company

Library of Congress Control Number: 2016938212

Edited by Sue Tate and Samantha Swenson
Designed by Five Seventeen
The artwork in this book was rendered in acrylic on gessoed board.
The text was set in P22 Stanyan.
Printed and bound in China

www.penguinrandomhouse.ca

1 2 3 4 5   21 20 19 18 17

Penguin
Random
House

TUNDRA BOOKS

To A. E. I. & "oh, you!" (Adara, Eli, Isaiah, and Jackson) —TB

For Amelia —BS

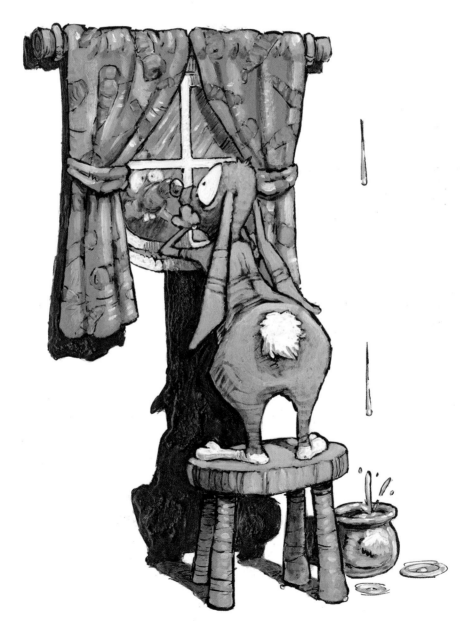

When a sudden, heavy rain
Spoiled the lovely summer weather
Two old friends had to remain
In the den they shared together.
"Rain is boring," sighed the hare.
Said the bear, "Poor thing!

There, there!"

"Rain goes on and on," Hare whined,
"It's been falling now for hours,
And I'm not a bit inclined
To put up with endless showers!"

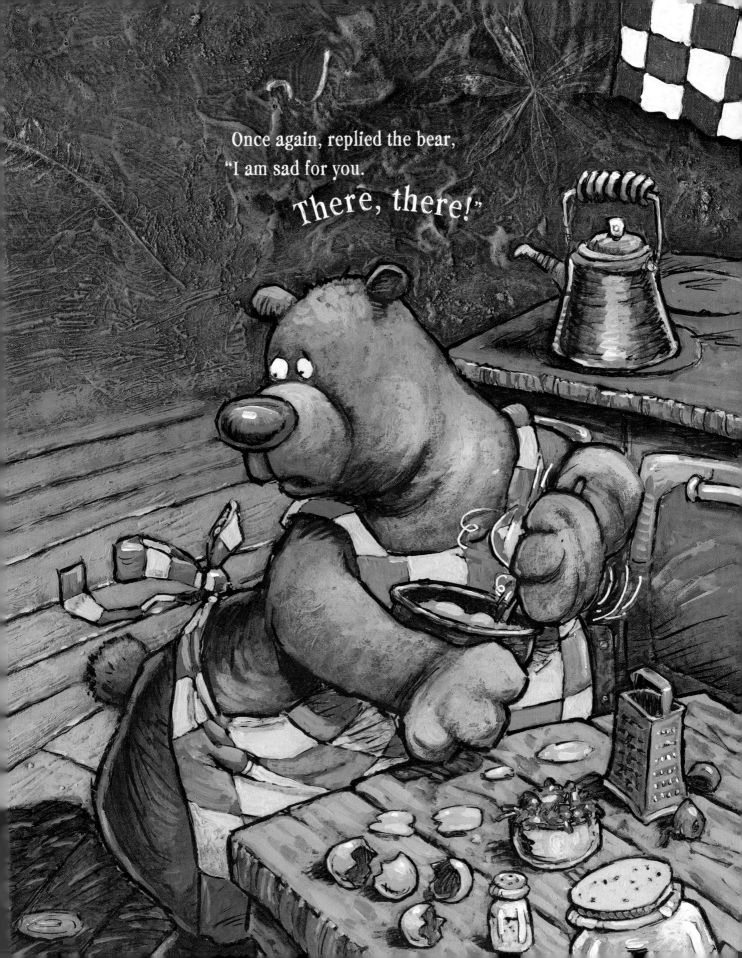

Once again, replied the bear,
"I am sad for you.

There, there!"

"I'm not having any fun!
I would rather be enjoying
Games and picnics in the sun.
Rainy days are so annoying!"
In a fit, Hare kicked a chair.
Said the bear, "Poor thing!
There, there!"

"OW, OW, OW!
I hurt my toe!"
Shrieked the hare, who started hopping
As big tears began to flow
Off his whiskers without stopping.

With an eye-roll said our bear,
"How you suffer so.

There, there!"

With a big, dramatic moan
On his bed the hare then tumbled.
"All along, I should have known
That you wouldn't care," he grumbled.

With his patience at an end,
"There, there, there, Hare!" growled his friend.

"And what's worse," our hare protested,
"Now the carrots have all molded!
And the cupboards are infested — "

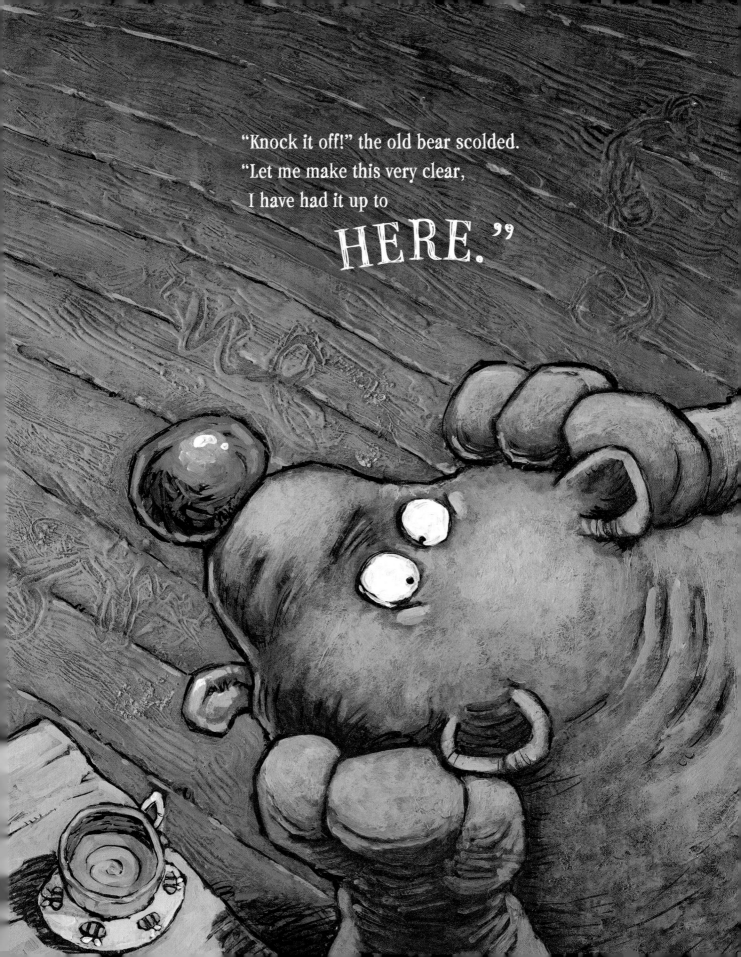

"Knock it off!" the old bear scolded.
"Let me make this very clear,
I have had it up to

HERE."

Then he dragged the hare outdoors
To a place where it was muddy,
And he got down on all fours.

"See this earthworm, little buddy?
If you think your life is grim,
Just be glad that you're not him."

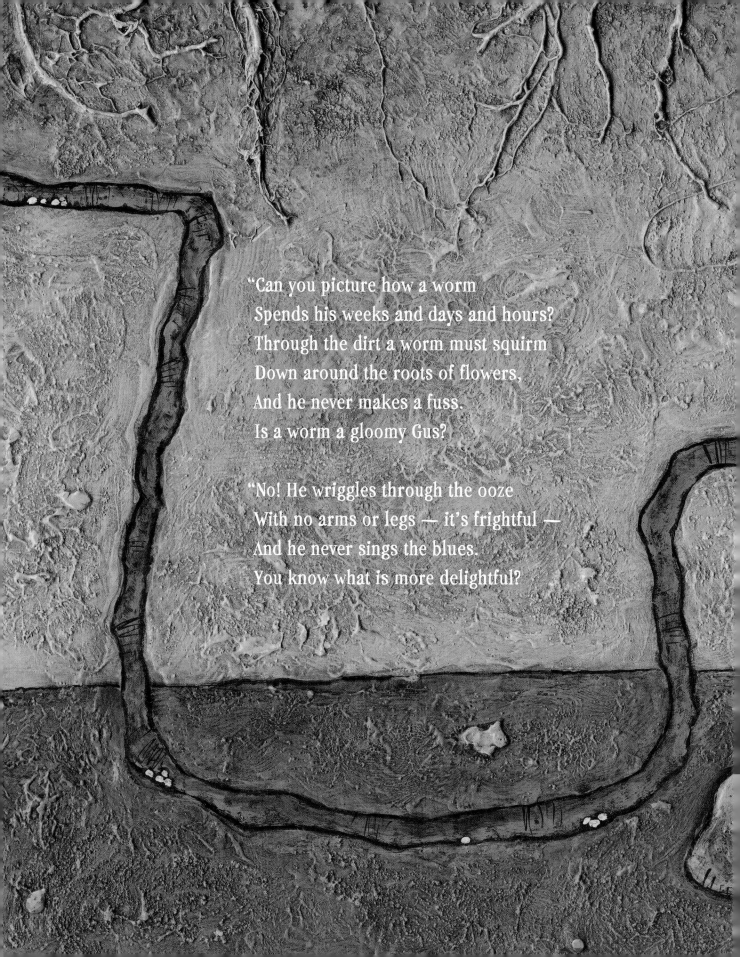

"Can you picture how a worm
Spends his weeks and days and hours?
Through the dirt a worm must squirm
Down around the roots of flowers,
And he never makes a fuss.
Is a worm a gloomy Gus?

"No! He wriggles through the ooze
With no arms or legs — it's frightful —
And he never sings the blues.
You know what is more delightful?

"When he meets his own rear end,
He mistakes it for a friend!"

In the mud, Hare sat and peered
At that poor, blind, wrinkled creature
Whose brown skin, all slimy-smeared,
Was his most attractive feature.
Hare compared the life he had,
And he thought, *Things aren't so bad.*

"Yes, I see," the hare then sighed.
"I have blessings by the plateful.
Take me home and we'll get dried,
And I'll try to be more grateful.
Bear, you're such a better friend
Than an earthworm's other end!"

All at once, the rainy day
Turned divinely warm and sunny,
So Bear tossed the worm away
And took home the soggy bunny.
But the worm down in the dirt
Had his feelings kind of hurt.

"How insulting to be used
By that bear in such a fashion.
To be pinched and dropped and bruised
With no kindness or compassion,
How upsetting! How unfair!"

Said his other end,

"There, there!"